Mesi's
SEASON OF CHANGE

A FRIENDSHIP STORY

PAM DAVIS
WITH KATHY BUCHANAN

Authentic

COLORADO SPRINGS • MILTON KEYNES • HYDERABAD

Authentic Publishing
We welcome your questions and comments.

USA   1820 Jet Stream Drive, Colorado Springs, CO 80921 www.authenticbooks.com
UK   9 Holdom Avenue, Bletchley, Milton Keynes, Bucks, MK1 1QR
        www.authenticmedia.co.uk
India   Logos Bhavan, Medchal Road, Jeedimetla Village, Secunderabad 500 055, A.P.

Mesi's Season of Change: A Friendship Story
ISBN-13: 978-1-934068-79-3
ISBN-10: 1-934068-79-9

Copyright © 2007 by Pam Davis

10 09 08 / 6 5 4 3 2 1

Illustrations: Monica Bucanelli
Cover/interior design: Julia Ryan/www.DesignByJulia.com
Editorial team: Kathy Buchanan, Diane Stortz, Michaela Dodd, Dan Johnson
Africa photos: © 2008 JupiterImages Corporation unless otherwise noted
Author photo: © Cliff Ranson, www.ransonphotography.com.
Some images: © 2008 iStockphoto.com, © 2008 JupiterImages Corporation

Printed in the United States of America

Contents

To my sons, Rhett and Rhys, with love.

May you—and all mothers' sons—choose Jesus and embrace his grace,

Then choose as your special mate a girl 'n grace.

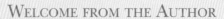

WELCOME FROM THE AUTHOR

Dear friends,

I am so pleased you are joining me as we journey through lives of girls in grace.

A Girl 'n Grace is a girl in whom the person of grace, Jesus Christ, lives. You'll notice there's a missing "I" and an apostrophe in its place. The Bible teaches that in order to live in a relationship with God one must surrender her life to Jesus. No longer do I live but rather it is Christ who lives in me as I live by faith in the Son of God (Galatians 2:20). A Girl 'n Grace is a girl who has surrendered her self-centered desires to the desires of Christ. In doing so, she discovers strength, satisfaction, and significance, which elevates her self-esteem and honors God.

Let this book aid you in discovering the desires of Jesus Christ, and may you, like these characters, proclaim, "I can through Christ."®

In his embrace,
Pam Davis
(ACTS 20:24)

Mesi (pronounced *Maycee*) is a girl growing up on the continent of Africa. The landscape is as diverse as its people and their beliefs. Through hardships, Mesi discovers a God who is near, so near that he cares about what concerns her. And she finds out about his inexhaustible treasure called grace.

Girls 'n Grace Place is a fun website where you can interact with the Girls 'n Grace characters.

You can. . .

join the free Reader's Club to take a quiz and win a prize! These heart-shaped icons in the book tell you there's a quiz question on the website.

participate with the Girls 'n Grace doll characters through a virtual experience and enjoy a wide range of activities: fashion, reader's club, travel, cooking, decorating, art, education, creating your own Girls 'n Grace magazine, and much more!

Visit the Girls 'n Grace characters at www.GirlsnGrace.com.

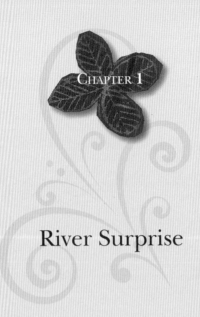

Chapter 1

River Surprise

"What's the capital of Egypt?" Mesi asked.

"Cairo," said Kwasi.

"What about Mexico?"

"Easy. Mexico City. My turn," Kwasi insisted.

Mesi sighed. She dreaded tomorrow's geography test. She wished she knew the answers as well as Kwasi, who liked nothing more than learning about the world beyond their small African village. Mesi, on the other hand, could hardly fathom ever being anywhere else.

She stuck out her arms to balance her way over the fallen tree limb that bridged the stream the girls crossed on their way home from school. The end of the rainy season was near, and the water roared underneath her, nearly escaping its banks. Today was muggy and hot, but it was no longer raining. That put both girls in a good mood.

"I hope I make a good score," Mesi said, now on the other side of the stream. She separated spider webs clinging to the thick vines in front of her, making a path for the girls to walk through. A snake slithered up the rough bark on a tree to her right. Mesi saw quickly it wasn't a poisonous snake. She'd been taught as a young child which snakes to avoid and which were safe.

Kwasi followed her under the dense canopy of foliage. "I know you will. Someday, Mesi, I'm going to go to all those places."

"Will you send me postcards?" Mesi asked.

"Of course. And chocolate."

Mesi grinned. She'd only sampled chocolate once in her life, but her best friend knew it was one of her favorite things in the world.

Drops of leftover rain trapped in the crevices of banana tree leaves dribbled down on their heads. Mesi clutched her assignment folder tightly to her chest to keep it from getting wet and silently thanked God once again for allowing her to go to school. Not everyone in her village could afford the uniform required to attend. She loved learning, and she was so grateful for the opportunity.

At the outskirts of their village, Mesi pointed out a clearing surrounded by red-frosted aloe plants taller than her.

"There's where Miss Ama and I want to build the church."

"How do you expect to build it? You don't have any materials," Kwasi said.

Mesi asked herself that question a lot. The village people struggled to come up with the cinder blocks, mortar, and tin sheets used to build their own homes. Some poorer villagers made mud huts covered with thatched grass roofs, but those so often had to be rebuilt after a windstorm or heavy rain.

"I don't know yet where we'll get everything. But I'm making money selling my doll clothes. Eventually I'll have enough to buy supplies."

Recently Mesi had met a woman in the city marketplace who owned a doll store in England. She paid Mesi to make doll clothes and ship them to her shop. The extra money paid for school.

Kwasi shook her head. "Do you know how long that will take? Years and years. And even after you buy the supplies, you still need to have them delivered here. How do you plan on doing that?"

Mesi chose not to respond. She didn't know all the answers. She only knew what was on her heart—to build a church, a safe place where people could meet her Jesus. Some of the villagers had heard Miss Ama discuss "spiritual gold"—her term for grace—with Mesi. They wondered if Mesi and Miss Ama were hiding nuggets of the precious metal somewhere in the village. Father told Mesi she needed to be careful how she spoke. But to Mesi, God's grace was far more valuable than actual gold.

They approached the three small, square buildings that made up Kwasi's homestead. Kwasi's mother was stoking the fire to cook the family's dinner of millet and yams.

"I'll need to do wash before dinner," Mesi said. "Should I come by and get you?"

"Yes. Mother will have plenty for me to do as well," Kwasi replied.

Mesi said goodbye to Kwasi and veered off toward her own home.

"You mustn't bother your father," Mother said as she tightened baby Jamilah onto her back with a wrapped blanket. "He's having an important meeting with the council. Kojo is finishing up at the field."

"Yes, Mother," Mesi replied. It wasn't unusual for her older brother, Kojo, to still be working after she returned from school.

Six men sat around the fire with her father. They spoke with concern. Mesi listened as she pounded grain. One of the men, Shabot, was clearly angry.

"I know those Kienese stole my boat. That's my livelihood. The livelihood of the village. If we can't fish, how will we eat?"

The other men nodded, and Mesi could see their furrowed brows. Shabot owned the only boat in the village, and this time of year her people depended on his fish to survive. It sounded like trouble was brewing again between her people, the Ashanti, and a neighboring tribe.

"First they say we stole the Ewus' gold and are hiding it, and now they steal our boat," continued Shabot. "Something needs to be done. We must speak to the Kienese."

"We need to approach them with fire and swords. They are an evil people. They have killed our people," said Mesi's uncle Yorkoo. His eyes glinted. "We have the power to bring destruction on their village. Now we will teach them not to steal boats."

"How do you know it was them?" Father asked.

"Who else would it be?" Yorkoo responded. "Kienese are

known for their lies and thieving ways. Remember the goats that disappeared a few years back?"

"I have more proof than that," said Shabot. "Three days ago I was downriver near their village, and two of the men called out to me. They wanted to buy the boat. They offered two cows."

"What did you tell them?" asked Chief Nbu.

"I said the boat wasn't for sale, that I needed it. And I told them if I did want to sell it, I would never sell it to a people who stole my great-great-grandfather's goats. Then I left. I didn't think of it again until I noticed the boat missing this morning."

"Well, that makes it clear enough. We should go to battle," said another village man, banging his walking stick on the ground in emphasis.

"Wait, wait. Perhaps if we talk to them . . . " Mesi's father said.

"Talk? What good is talking to that village?" asked Uncle Yorkoo. "They are vicious people. They speak with their spears, not listen with their ears."

"We still have to give them a chance," said Chief Nbu, agreeing with Father.

Uncle Yorkoo noticed Mesi pounding the grain. "Mesi, bring me some water."

"Yes, Uncle Yorkoo," she said.

"And how is that church coming along now? Are you ready for the roof yet?" His voice was mocking.

Mesi bit her lip. When she'd told Uncle Yorkoo about God's wonderful grace and that she wanted to build a church, he'd shaken his head and said she was living with her head in the clouds. And now, weeks later, he still jabbed at her with his sarcastic remarks.

Father, on the other hand, had said he liked the idea of a church, despite his warnings that it would be nearly impossible for the village to afford. He said he'd seen a change in Mesi, a light in her eyes when she spoke of the gift in her heart. He'd even suggested that a church could be used as a community center—a place to hold celebrations protected from the rain and perhaps to store grain.

But when Uncle Yorkoo heard this, he'd thrown back his head and laughed, displaying his rotted two front teeth—the result of his sugar cane-chewing habit.  He was constantly gnawing on a stalk. "Certainly. In fifty years when we have the things to build it, it shall be a very good community center." Mesi felt like she had been slapped.

But now, as Mesi started to get Uncle Yorkoo's water, Mother came to her rescue. "Mesi, go ahead and take the wash down to the river. I'll serve the water."

Mesi took the tied bundle of clothes and blankets from her mother and balanced it on her head. She was thankful to get away as she strode off down the still-muddy path, her bare feet leaving sticky footprints.

She waved to Miss Ama, who was tending her small garden.

"Ah, you have anger etched on your gentle face, dear Mesi."

Gray-haired Miss Ama, known as the village sage, always seemed to know what she was thinking. Mesi adored Miss Ama, and she felt embarrassed that her anger was so obvious.

"Uncle Yorkoo doesn't believe in the riches of God's grace. He doesn't think we will ever build a church. He mocks me every time he sees me."

"Ah, a doubter indeed," Miss Ama said with a nod. "You shall come across many."

"If I ever get that church built, I hope he never comes inside," Mesi muttered. "That would show him."

Miss Ama smiled. She had a smile that took up her whole face, transforming it into a series of gentle creases. She nodded toward a tree down the path. "Do you see Matala up there?"

Mesi looked up into the tall tree where a young man from the village was plucking dates. Matala noticed them looking at him and waved.

"No good tree bears bad fruit, nor does a bad tree bear good fruit. Each tree is recognized by its own fruit," said Miss Ama. "That is what God says in his Word."

Mesi knew Miss Ama was trying to tell her something, but she had no idea what. Was she supposed to go pick dates alongside Matala?

Miss Ama continued to gaze up at the huge feathery leaves topping the tree. "You are being transformed by God's grace, Mesi. You are a good tree. And to show that you are a good tree, you will bear good fruit."

Mesi began to understand. "Good fruit? Like gentleness and kindness, right?"

"Yes," said Miss Ama. "And love and patience."

Mesi sighed. She understood now. "So I should not try to keep Uncle Yorkoo from coming into the church?"

Miss Ama's gaze traveled from the treetop to Mesi's brown eyes. "To refrain from punishing him would be mercy. But there is more than mercy. God gave us grace. So, yes, extend your uncle grace. Invite him to God's church."

Mesi pondered this. "I should show kindness and patience to him, even when he makes fun of me?"

Miss Ama nodded.

"Then he will be among the first I invite to our—I mean, *God's*—church," Mesi said.

"That, my dear, is beautiful fruit."

Mesi walked away considering Miss Ama's words. She didn't want to be kind to Uncle Yorkoo, but she knew Miss Ama was right. Miss Ama was always right.

Kwasi waved as Mesi approached the homestead. She spoke quickly to her mother, ducked into one of the small one-room huts, and came out with her own bundle of wash. She set the load on her head and pranced out to see Mesi. Kwasi always seemed to have a dance in her step. Mesi admired how her friend had such strength but still moved with the ease of a gazelle.

The girls giggled about things that had happened at school that day as they made their way under cabbage trees and river bushwillows—also known as hiccup nut trees, because eating their nuts would result in a bad case of hiccups.  Ten minutes later they came to a widened place in the river where the current slowed. They undid their bundles and started scrubbing clothes and blankets with bars of soap, draping each finished item on overhanging branches to dry in the warm sun.

Kwasi started singing an old African ballad, and Mesi added her own voice. They'd been harmonizing throughout nearly the entire load of laundry when Kwasi suddenly stopped.

"Wait. Do you hear that?" she asked Mesi.

Mesi strained to listen for anything other than the sounds of rushing water and the distant calls of the kingfisher birds. A deep moaning came from somewhere close. An animal of some sort, perhaps? Mesi couldn't think what. She instinctively tightened her muscles to spring into a run should something jump out at them.

Kwasi, her eyes wide, pointed behind Mesi. Mesi turned slowly, wondering if she'd see a crocodile slithering out of the water or a lion glaring at them with its claws bared. But it was neither. It was even more surprising! There, splayed on the shore behind some overgrown brush, were feet . . . boy's feet!

The groaning proved the boy was alive, but what condition was he in? The girls ran over and pulled away sticks and leaves.

A boy about their age, in drenched, torn clothes, peered out at them through half-closed eyes. Scratches covered his face, and deep gashes lined his arms.

Mesi didn't think she'd ever seen the boy before. "Are you all right?" Mesi asked.

"I'm in pain," the boy answered, barely moving his mouth. He took a breath that seemed to be excruciating. "Went hunting upriver. A boar charged me. Fell off cliff into river and swept down here."

Mesi remembered her uncle Thando broke half his ribs when he was attacked by a boar. The boy held his side the same way her uncle had. "You probably broke some bones," she said.

"I can't get up. I grabbed this vine and barely pulled myself to shore." The boy's hand was still wrapped around the scraggly vine, his lifeline.

"We'll help you. What's your name?" asked Mesi.

"Numu. I'm from the Kienese village."

Kienese. Mesi swallowed hard as she grasped what that meant. At her feet, half-dead, lay the enemy.

CHAPTER 2

War of Generations

Kwasi grabbed Mesi's hand and pulled her close. "We can't help him," she murmured. "Let's run and tell the council."

"But they'll kill him," Mesi said.

Kwasi looked at the boy and shrugged. "He probably deserves it."

Mesi saw the boy's face contorted in pain. He reminded her of her brother, Kojo, who only a few short months ago had been injured in a fire. If he'd been found hurt by others, she'd have wanted them to help him. She couldn't allow angry Shabot or any of the men in the village to know about Numu. They would do horrible things to him.

Mesi shook her head, her decision made. "I can't do that. I can't tell them!"

Kwasi looked again at the boy, who was watching them, trying to decipher what they were whispering.

"Remember how badly Kojo was hurt," Mesi said. "What if he were lying here at the feet of the Kienese?"

13

Perhaps it was Mesi's pleading that finally softened Kwasi's heart. "I suppose we could just leave him here," she said. "His people will find him eventually. He'll be better off staying."

Mesi was thankful. He was safer injured in the wilderness than in their village. But still . . . it seemed so cruel to just leave the boy here. Numu clearly needed help. At least some food to eat. And what if an animal found him? Lions roamed along the river all the time.

"C'mon." Kwasi pulled on Mesi's arm. "Let's go. You've done your kind deed."

Mesi tugged back. Kind deed . . . Miss Ama's words came back to her. *To refrain from punishing him would be mercy. But there is more than mercy. God gave us grace.* Mercy would be to leave the boy here, and perhaps he would be found soon. But grace required something more. Grace would mean carrying the boy to safety. Grace would mean caring for him.

The boy still watched her—his face a mixture of pain and fear. "You're Ashanti, aren't you?" he muttered.

"Yes. And we can't help you," said Kwasi through gritted teeth.

The boy closed his eyes. "I didn't know I'd come that far." He sounded defeated, without hope. He'd die by either the hands of the Ashanti or the teeth of wild animals. He struggled to get up again but fell down flat.

"We're taking him with us," said Mesi.

"What? Now you want to hand him over to Shabot?"

"No, we're going to hide him in Lulu's shack." That was the first safe place that came to mind. Kojo had recently rebuilt their cow's lean-to. Mesi was in charge of feeding and milking the cow. No one else hardly ever went into the shack.

"You can't be serious," said Kwasi.

"I'm very serious," said Mesi.

Kwasi's eyes stared wide as she slowly shook her head. Mesi half expected her to run into the jungle.

"As my friend, Kwasi. Please," Mesi pleaded.

Kwasi shrugged. "Because you are a sister," she said, "I will help you take him to the shack, but I will have nothing more to do with him after that."

Kwasi took one of the still-damp blankets off the tree branch. The two girls carefully lifted the Kienese boy onto the blanket. He groaned with every centimeter of movement. Then Mesi picked up one side of the blanket and Kwasi the other. They would come back for the rest of the laundry tomorrow afternoon, after it had dried.

The girls moved down the jungle path silently, listening to Numu's pained murmurings. Mesi tried to be as careful as possible, moving slowly and avoiding rocky pathways.

"He's getting heavy," Kwasi complained.

"We're almost there."

The cow shack stood on the edge of the family's cocoa field, beyond the perimeter of the village. There wasn't a door on the shack, so Mesi shooed Lulu out without needing to release the blanket. She kicked some hay into the middle of the dirt floor, and the girls placed Numu down in the center of it.

"I'm leaving now, Mesi," Kwasi said. She looked both ways outside the shack to see if they'd been seen. "I'll talk to you later, but not about this." She gestured to the crumpled body at her feet as if the boy were a pile of spilled millet.

Mesi followed Kwasi outside and tied the cow to a tree.

"He's a person, Kwasi," she said. "We couldn't leave him."

"We *could* leave him. We could have turned him in to the tribal elders. If you cared about the village at all, that's what you would have done." Fire danced in Kwasi's eyes. "And maybe that's what I should still do," she muttered under her breath.

Mesi did care about the village, but she also knew she couldn't let this boy lie starving on the side of the river. "Give me some time to help him."

Kwasi's arms flailed. "Why should you help him? His people killed my grandfather. They stole our goats. They've threatened this village. And now they've stolen our boat so we can't get fish these next few months. Those fish keep my little brother and sister alive. Is this boy's life more important than theirs?"

"But it wasn't him," Mesi said. Mesi knew Kwasi had heard those stories of the Kienese since she was born. Like the other villagers, Kwasi believed you carried the works of your ancestors with you. Their glories and successes, as well as their sins and failures, were as much a part of you as your own actions. You were named for the family that preceded you and defined by the character of your bloodline. There was nothing good about a Kienese boy in Kwasi's eyes and nothing Mesi could do to change that. "I don't know what his ancestors have done," she said, "but he's never hurt us."

Kwasi stared at her.

"And even if he did hurt us," Mesi continued, "it doesn't mean we need to hurt him back."

Kwasi just shook her head, turned, and hurried off toward the village.

Mesi didn't know if Kwasi would tell the village elders or not and said a quick prayer that she wouldn't. For her friend this was more about loyalty than compassion. She hoped Kwasi would choose to be loyal to her rather than the village.

"You haven't eaten much tonight," Mother said. She looked at Mesi's tin plate. A mound of millet covered with beans still filled the plate. "Are you feeling all right?"

Mesi felt the concern of her mother's eyes. She didn't want her mother to worry about her coming down with any-thing. During malaria season swarms of mosquitoes could cover them for days. Now the rainy months were ending, and the insects had gravitated away from the village and reconvened by the river. Mesi hardly noticed the annoying bugs anymore, but they could carry malaria, a deadly disease. "I don't feel sick, Mother," she said. "I'm just not very hungry. I must've eaten a large breakfast."

Mother tilted her head quizzically. Their meals were never large.

It was true that Mesi didn't feel hungry. She was too nervous to eat. But, besides that, she wanted to leave some food to bring to Numu.

"I'll finish it off," she said. As Mother turned to tend the baby, Mesi poured clumps of moist grain into one of the side pockets of her dress. She had a long piece of narrow cloth in the other. After helping Mother with the dishes, she excused herself to go feed the cow.

"I heard you talking to your friend," Numu said. He lay on his side, wolfing down the millet. Mesi wondered how long it had been since he had eaten.

"She may tell the elders," Mesi said. "But I hope not."

Numu stopped eating and looked at her, his brown eyes still showing that he did not completely trust her. "Why did you save me? Your people and my people have been enemies for generations."

Mesi didn't know where to start, so she opted for the simple answer. "Grace."

"What?"

 Mesi took a deep breath. "I've been given mercy and grace—forgiveness and good- ness—from God. And because of that, I want to give those to others. I believe that's what God would want me to do. And I want to please him because he loves me so much."

"I've never heard of a god like that," Numu said.

"I know. Many of my people haven't either."

He looked at her uncomfortably. "Don't gods bring enemies to us so we can hurt them?"

"Not my God," Mesi said. "He brings them to me so I can show kindness."

"Your god doesn't make sense."

"Perhaps not," Mesi answered. "But that's what I think makes him so great."

She knew God was different from any other gods in Africa. There were gods, spirits of ancestors—even animals— believed to bring rain, health, or gold. But the gods were all changeable, moody, and difficult to please. If the people danced before one god to get rain for the crops and rain didn't come, they'd go before another. You could do many things to spur the gods' anger—killing certain animals, neglecting a holiday, dishonoring a sacred space. The villagers constantly tried to please all the so-called gods around them in hopes of getting what they wanted and lived in fear of breaking any of the sacred traditions.

Mesi had found freedom from trying to please all these gods. Still, it was difficult sometimes to wrap her mind around the idea of a God who loved her, a God who wanted to do good things for her even when she wasn't good.

Mesi held up Numu's head to help him drink some water. Then she took out the long, narrow piece of cloth she'd brought and wrapped it around his ribs.

Numu sighed. "Much better. Thank you," he murmured. His eyes were closed as he lay on the mat, and Mesi thought he'd fallen asleep. She covered him with an extra blanket and started to leave.

But he spoke again, his eyes still closed. "Why do you think our people fight so much?"

Mesi knew what most would say. At least what she'd been told since the time she was a tiny girl. She'd heard all the stories and was sure Numu had too. The trouble began generations ago with a fight over water rights to certain parts of the river. One tribe attacked the other, and the other retaliated. But she knew Numu's question went beyond that. Why were they *still* enemies? What good was it doing? "I don't know," she answered. "I wish I did."

Numu's eyes opened. "Do you play soccer?"

Mesi nodded. Everyone in her village played soccer. Her brother was thought to be one of the best players.

"That's what I would be doing if I were home right now. With my friends—"

Shhh. Mesi motioned with a finger to her mouth. Heavy steps sounded beyond the thin shack's walls. The flimsy stick sides rustled as though someone had brushed against them. Someone was out there.

Numu could hear it too. The whites of his eyes grew larger, shining like the headlights of a mammy wagon, trucks that carried people and animals. "Who is it?" he whispered.

"I'll go see," Mesi whispered back. She couldn't swallow. She pictured a group of men from the village, having just heard the news from Kwasi, circling around the shack to get Numu. What would they do to him?

Gingerly, she stepped out into the night. A cloud wandered in front of the moon, making the night blacker than black. She could barely see her hand in front of her face—but she could sense the movement, hear the breathing.

In the distance, night calls echoed into the inky sky. The monkeys were starting their evening activities. But someone was closer and coming behind her with heavy footsteps. Something tickled her arm. She spun around.

Moooo.

"Lulu!" Mesi laughed and gasped at the same time. The cow had gotten loose from the tree where she'd been tied. Mesi took a deep breath.

"Is everything okay?" Numu called.

"Yes," Mesi said. She tied up Lulu again and went back inside.

"I thought warriors were surrounding us," said Numu.

"Me too. Or maybe a giant rhinoceros with a horn as sharp as a Zulu spear and legs as thick as tree trunks."

Numu chuckled. "You sound like my uncles and grand-father as they sit around the fire, sharing stories. The same stories every night."

Mesi smiled. It was like evenings at her homestead. "My uncle Banta, uncle Yorkoo, and Chief Nbu do that too. They'll talk about the rhinoceros they killed with one broken arrow."

 "Or the elephant that nearly trampled them before they climbed a banana tree."

"Or the black mamba snake that jumped out at them—"

"And quick as lightning they caught it by its tail and swung it into the jungle," Numu finished for her.

"Yes!" Mesi said. "And doesn't that snake keep getting longer every time the story is told?"

"It does," said Numu. "And the rhinoceros gets bigger. I half expect that next time it will tower over the banana trees and eat grass huts in a single gulp."

"We've been hearing the same stories then!" Mesi laughed.

Numu joined in, holding his ribs in pain. "Stop. Laughing hurts too much."

Mesi's eyes exposed her smile though she shielded her mouth with her hand. "I'll be serious then," she promised.

"Is the cow tied up again?" he asked.

"Yes. She should be fine for the night. I'll move her to a grassier spot when I come to milk her in the morning."

"You tend the cow?" Numu said. "That is an important task."

Mesi knew that was true. It wasn't often a young girl like herself had responsibility for taking care of such a valuable

21

commodity. The number of cows a family owned—if any at all—was a measure of its wealth. "I have been given another important task," she confided. "God has asked me to build his church."

Numu's eyes widened. "By yourself?"

 Mesi laughed. "Well, I wouldn't build it alone. But I want to make it happen. First, though, I need to get cinder blocks. Not easy, of course."

"You're going to build a church? That's not even possible," Numu said.

"If both our uncles can kill the same rhinoceros, *anything* is possible."

Numu laughed with her again, wrapping his arms around his ribs. "If you make me laugh anymore, I'll never heal," he joked.

Despite Numu's newly jovial mood, Mesi wondered how long it would take Numu to heal—or if he even would. When Kojo was badly hurt, she and her mother took him to the city hospital to see a doctor. Mesi glanced at the hay they were sitting on. This shack was no hospital, and she was no doctor.

As if Numu could read her worried look, he said, "Once I recover a little, I'll hike back to my village. It should just be a day or two."

Mesi didn't say anything. Numu was weeks away from being able to walk that far. He was like a wounded elk near a den of lions. The villagers would discover him in time. Tonight it was only Lulu knocking. Tomorrow it could be Shabot. Mesi shuddered at the thought. She'd enjoyed talking to Numu tonight. She imagined he would be a friend of hers if they were from the same village. *But we aren't,* she reminded herself.

A sudden chill swept over her. "I must be going."

Mesi withdrew into the darkness outside the shack and headed back to the village, a full moon lighting the way.

♡♡♡

Mesi could see faint reflections darting off the leaves of the banana trees. She realized she hadn't seen a moon like that in months. The rains had kept it hidden.

Mesi considered how she could return Numu to his village. There was no way she could do this on her own. She would have to tell her father about him. Certainly he would help. The people would see Numu was a boy like the ones in their village—he wasn't scary or threatening.

A mysterious glow appeared beyond the trees ahead of her. She stopped to watch. The shadows shifted in response to a flickering light. Then in the clearing appeared a band of tribal elders, each bearing a lit torch. Shabot led the way. Mesi leaned against a tree, hoping to escape being seen. But nothing missed Shabot's eagle eyes.

"Girl! What are you doing out at night?"

"Checking on the cow," she explained. That was partially true.

"It's too late for you to be out," Shabot said. "We are entering a time of battle. The Kienese could be hiding around these trees right now, waiting to pounce on us, ready to kill us."

23

Mesi's heart dropped. The only Kienese she knew of close by was too injured to pounce, but certainly in a place where he could be killed.

"We are on our way to speak to the Kienese now," another village man spoke. "We will tell them that they need to return the boat, or we will go to battle."

"And if we find any in the woods spying on us on our way, we will take care of them as well," Shabot muttered.

The village had lived in peace as long as Mesi remembered, but she'd heard the stories of previous battles: of the night attacks, the abduction of women and children, the men with streaks of red and gold painted across their cheeks, forehead, and chest. Many of them trained to run miles in a day, outrace galloping horses, and kill with a single arrow.

The troop disappeared into the jungle, and Mesi could see the fire in front of her homestead through the branches. She'd planned on telling her father about Numu, but now she wasn't so sure. The elders would be thrilled to learn they had a hostage already, and she feared for Numu's life.

She didn't know how long it would take Numu to heal or how he would get back to his village. But as she ducked into her hut, she determined there was one thing she *did* know. She was not going to tell anyone about him.

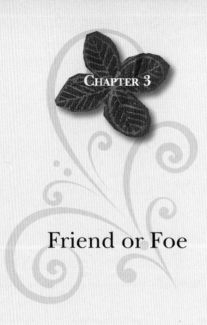

CHAPTER 3

Friend or Foe

"I wish I hadn't made that promise to you, Mesi, because I'd have made sure everyone knew by now." As Kwasi walked with Mesi to school, she urged Mesi to tell the people in the village about Numu. "How long do you think you can keep this a secret?" Kwasi continued.

Mesi shrugged. She didn't know. This morning, when she went to milk Lulu, Numu had still been asleep—his long limbs askew over the edges of the blanket—oblivious to the growing enmity between their villages and the risk to his life.

Last night in bed, holding her treasured doll, Toolie, close, she'd prayed. She asked God to show her what to do next. No voice came from heaven. She considered visiting Miss Ama and telling her about Numu, but it was disrespectful for a child to call on someone of Miss Ama's stature uninvited.

"I wonder what happened last night when the men visited the Kienese." Mesi carefully walked around a muddy patch.

"I'm sure we will hear when we get home."

♡ ♡ ♡

The two-room school was a cinder block building with a cement floor. The children in primary classes met in one room, and the children who continued past level eight met in the other, smaller room.

Mesi struggled to pay attention while Miss Latama reviewed the spelling words for tomorrow's test. Her thoughts were preoccupied with visions of a looming battle. She thought again of the stories of painted warriors racing with lit torches through the village, setting the thatched buildings on fire, and plundering the rest.

"Mesi?" Miss Latama tapped on her desk with a ruler. Mesi had been staring out the window at the dirt field the children used as a playground. "Would you care to spell *consensus*?"

Mesi did *not* care to, actually, but that wasn't an option. "Yes, ma'am," she said, standing up from her desk to answer the question. "C-O-N-C-E-N-S-U-S. Consensus."

"That is incorrect. I suggest you pay attention if you want to do better than that on the test tomorrow."

Mesi forced herself to watch the front of the room with her hands clasped on her desk, as was expected. She'd escaped punishment, but her teacher would not be so merciful next time. Mesi was relieved when Miss Latama finally dismissed the class.

Kwasi and Mesi talked with their friends in the schoolyard. Some played with their cornhusk dolls that had been tucked inside their burlap sacks all day. Others brought out treasured crayons and bouncy balls to share. One of the boys showed them a truck he'd made of old wire. Most of the other boys played soccer with a half-inflated ball. Mesi found herself wondering what Numu's school was like—would his friends be doing the same things hers were?

Auntie Loita clicked her tongue as she passed the girls on the village outskirts. Her head held a large basket piled high with bananas. "Mesi, your mother has been looking for you."

Mesi said a quick goodbye to Kwasi and sped up her pace. She knew she'd played too long after school. She hoped only her tardiness was concerning Mother and not that Numu had been found in the cow shack.

"We need to hurry with dinner," Mother said when Mesi reached the homestead. "Father has a meeting with the council soon. Take Jamilah for a while." Mesi's heart pounded as she tied her sister onto her back with a blanket. The council was meeting unexpectedly? What did it mean? Something must have happened.

Mesi hurried through her chores like never before. At the river retrieving water, she saw Kwasi and rushed toward her. "Do you have many chores?" she asked.

"No," Kwasi said. "But I am not going to visit that boy with you."

"I want you to hide with me during the council meeting. I need to find out what happened last night."

Kwasi tilted her head. Mesi knew nothing intrigued her as much as a little adventure. "I suppose I could do that," Kwasi said.

The meeting would take place behind Chief Nbu's house, around a large stone fire ring surrounded by a wide circle of cedar benches. Mesi tightened the blanket that wrapped around her waist and held her baby sister on her back. She hoped Mother wouldn't expect her to take care of Jamilah tonight. They'd be found out for sure if the baby started crying or gurgling during the meeting.

After dinner Mesi cleaned up the dishes, wrapped some food in a cloth for Numu, and hurried to Kwasi's homestead. She could already see the smoke coming from the fire behind Chief Nbu's house. The meeting would be starting soon.

The girls ran into the thick part of the jungle and circled around to the outskirts of the clearing. They crawled on their hands and knees through the tall grasses, keeping watch for the many snakes that made their home there.

"You're rustling the reeds too much," Kwasi hissed.

Mesi forced herself to move slower. The men were trained hunters. They would see even the slightest movement. They hoped the dusk would hide them.

The girls finally got in close. Mesi could smell the fire and hear the men talking. Suddenly, Chief Nbu quieted them. Mesi spread the grasses in front of her to give her a view of what was going on. Next to her Kwasi did the same.

"Baka is here from the Kienese village," Chief Nbu said. He stood next to a man who reminded Mesi of a reed, very thin and taller than any man she'd ever seen. He wore bedraggled tan pants and a white shirt, and he was barefoot.

Baka nodded to the men and then worked his way around the circle, extending his hand to each man. The men responded by standing up and returning his handshake with their left hand under their right elbow—a customary sign of respect. The young Kienese man bowed his head slightly to each man, demonstrating his honor as he greeted them by saying, "*Akwaba.*"

Shabot did not return Baka's handshake. He remained sitting on the bench, arms crossed and eyes averted.

Baka stood in front of the men and cleared his throat. The fire flickered at his bare feet. "Ashanti men, I come to you humbly. We received your messengers last night, and my chief sent me to you to extend a hand of peace. We do not wish to fight you. We have not stolen the boat you speak of. Chief Maku has questioned everyone carefully. He feels your accusations are unfounded. We wish for you to find your boat."

Shabot stood up. "We wish for that as well, Baka. We were hoping you could be of help." His even tone displayed no sarcasm, but his expression told everyone he did not believe the Kienese were innocent.

"I assure you that we have stolen nothing. You see, my people are in grief." Baka looked down at his feet.

"Why is that, Baka?" Chief Nbu asked.

"The son of our chief is missing. He went hunting six days ago and never returned. We came across tracks on a cliff over the river north of here. It appears he was forced into the water by a wild animal. We've searched the river but found nothing."

"Please pass on our sympathies to your chief," Chief Nbu said. The other men murmured their agreement.

Mesi felt a sharp jab in the ribs.

"Numu," Kwasi mouthed.

Mesi nodded.

"Our chief still believes his son to be alive. The boy is a good swimmer, but most likely quite injured. If you see him or traces of where he has been—anything—please, let us know. We would be so grateful."

The other men nodded, casting quick glances at each other. Mesi knew how to read them. The men had as little belief that this boy who'd been missing for nearly a week was still alive as they had belief in the innocence of the Kienese.

"I must go now," Baka said. His lanky body bent down to shake hands again. As before, Shabot refused.

The whole interaction had been orderly and quiet, but chaos erupted once Baka was out of earshot.

"Innocent!" Shabot threw his head back with a laugh. "If they were so innocent, the gods wouldn't have taken away the chief's son."

Mesi's father raised his eyebrows. "So you feel his disappearance is a sign of the gods' punishment?"

"Of course," answered an older man as he pounded his walking stick into the dirt. "And you can't believe a word those Kienese say. If they say right, the answer is left. If they say yes, the answer is no."

"I believe Baka may be sincere," Chief Nbu said.

A roar of protest arose. Uncle Yorkoo's voice shouted louder than the rest. "With all due respect, Chief Nbu, we all  know that's what the Kienese are known for. They put on appearances. But they are not who they say. They are an evil people."

A chorus of agreement rang out, but Mesi noticed her father chose not to participate.

"But I shall tell you this," Shabot said. "If I did find his son alive, he would soon wish he wasn't."

Kwasi leaned in closer to Mesi. "We need to go. It's getting very late."

The moon was rising in the sky, and Mesi nodded. As much as she wanted to hear the rest of the meeting, she still needed to bring Numu his dinner.

"Have you thought of the possibility that Numu might be a spy?" Kwasi asked once they'd crawled out of the grasses and were back into the jungle.

"You heard Baka. He disappeared," Mesi said.

"And you heard the elders," she said. "If a Kienese says right, the real answer is left. They're not honest people."

♡ ♡ ♡

"I didn't know if you would come today," Numu said as he stuffed the millet into his mouth. "I was getting hungry."

"Sorry I'm late," Mesi said.

Numu shook his head. "You do not have anything to apologize for. I still owe you my life."

"Your life isn't safe until we get you home." Mesi remembered what Shabot had said about what would happen if he found the boy. Numu needed to get home as soon as possible.

He sat up the tiniest bit. "Look, I'm able to sit up some. I'm getting better."

Mesi nodded. *But not quickly enough,* she thought. "It will be a long time before you are well enough to walk all the way back to your village. We need to come up with another way."

"The only other way would be by water. Do you have a boat?"

"There are no boats around. There was only one in the village and it was . . . stolen." She chose not to share the controversy about who had stolen it. There was no sense upsetting Numu.

"And there are no others?" asked Numu.

"No," Mesi said.

"No problem," he said. "Then we will just take your airplane." He began to laugh, his white teeth gleaming in the night.

"Of course." Mesi laughed at the thought. She'd only seen airplanes in the air or in pictures.

Numu leaned back and exhaled a long breath. "Don't worry, friend. We will think of something."

"Yes, we will," Mesi agreed. But what? She could push him in a wheelbarrow, but that would take so long. The jungle would surely trap it in mud every few feet. Perhaps she could build a raft, but that would take weeks, and the current was too fast to be safe.

Then she remembered.

"Numu, I think I might have thought of a way."

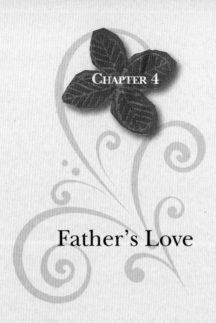

CHAPTER 4

Father's Love

Mesi dragged out the old raft from under a wall of gnarled brush. The sticks making up the raft were held tightly together with cords. It wasn't much. Kojo had used it for spearfishing last year, but it was in such bad shape he gave up on it and decided to make another one. He never started the new one because of his injury.

A stick broke off from the back as Mesi pulled the raft out a little farther. Would it make it downriver? Looking at it now, her doubts increased. Even in the raft's best days, it had only been used a few yards offshore, never to travel several kilometers downstream. But at this point her options were limited.

She tightened up the cords and added more twine and a few new sticks along the edges. Then she pulled out a jar of tree sap she'd collected and began to fill the spaces between the sticks.

Numu grimaced and held his injured ribs tight as he limped down to the water. He certainly wouldn't be able to walk much farther.

"What do you think?" Mesi asked, pointing at the raft lying on the riverbank.

"You really think this will make it?"

Mesi shrugged. "I hope so. We'll have to be careful."

"Very careful," Numu said.

The water rushed next to them, reminding them the river was still high and moving quite fast this time of year.

"I'll need your help steering it, making sure we don't hit any rocks," Mesi said. "Are you able to do that?"

Numu nodded. "I can do that. I have done it many times."

Numu had told Mesi about spearfishing with his uncles. Apparently, he was exceptionally gifted at it.

He also had experience in maneuvering the boats. Of course, Mesi was certain none of the boats were nearly as haphazard as this raft.

Gingerly, Numu reached down for a thick stick about four feet long. "This will do for steering." He winced with pain as he picked it up and examined it.

"Then we'll leave first thing in the morning," Mesi said.

"That is good," Numu said. He looked at her. "Are you worried, Mesi?"

"A little," she admitted. "But I believe God will watch over us."

"Your god will protect us, you think?" He considered this.

"Should we make a sacrifice to him before we leave?"

Mesi shook her head. "My God isn't like that."

"I don't think I'll ever understand your god," said Numu.

♡♡♡

The sky glowed with pinks and oranges. Mesi clutched the handkerchief with millet and yams she'd packed for lunch. The water danced down the riverbed, splashing up white sprays at every rock.

Numu stood next to her. "It looks faster than yesterday," he said.

"Yes, but maybe it's because now we're actually getting into it."

Mesi said a quick, silent prayer, asking God to keep them safe on their journey. A ray of the rising sun illuminated the pathway the raft would take. She took that as a sign. It was time to go.

The two silently pushed the raft into the water and waded in after it, the water swirling around their knees. Mesi climbed on and helped Numu on after her. Lying on her stomach, Mesi could feel the rickety sticks jolt and shift under her legs. She prayed again. *Lord, please keep this raft together.*

Numu sat up, staying as low as he could to keep the raft balanced, and pushed the raft away from the shore. He was quite skilled at avoiding the rocks and rapids. The sun had risen higher, and Mesi felt its warmth on her back. Her body began to relax, and for the first time she realized how tense she must have been. Now she felt safe with Numu steering the boat. "This might work," Mesi said.

"Perhaps your god is watching out for us after all," Numu replied.

"God doesn't belong to me, Numu. I belong to him. He is my Father."

"Oh . . . it is the spirit of your father, then—this god," Numu said.

"No, my earthly father is still alive. God is my heavenly Father." A wave splashed up over the raft and drenched her left side. "He loves us like our fathers on earth love us and protect us," she continued.

Numu smiled at the thought of being reunited with his father. "I know my father is searching everywhere for me right now. He will not give up. He will always hope that I return safely."

"And that is how God is," Mesi insisted.

Numu leaned back to think about this. The river took a bend, and the raft swerved. Numu didn't notice the set of rapids coming up. They seemed to come from nowhere.

"The rocks, Numu!" Mesi warned.

But it was too late. The edge of the raft hit a large boulder under the water. The corner veered up. Mesi flew off the raft and landed in the water.

She shook herself off, stunned, and then flailed her arms to stay afloat. The raft continued to move downstream.

"Hang on!" Numu called. "I'll stop the raft."

She watched him desperately try to guide the raft to shore, but the rocks along the sides of the river kept it in the current.

Mesi wasn't a very good swimmer, but the current helped push her along, and she grasped onto rocks from time to time to keep herself afloat. About fifty meters up, she saw that Numu had grabbed onto an overhanging vine and pulled the raft closer to shore.

He waved. Then his happy face quickly turned to horror. "Mesi!" he screamed, pointing behind her.

She held tight to a rock and glanced behind her. A lump formed in her throat. Two heavily lidded eyes slowly moved toward her. *Crocodile!* Mesi had never seen one this close before. She could make out its scaly skin. Its eyes were intent on her. She wondered briefly if this was the last thing she would ever see.

Without even thinking, Mesi let go of the rock and began kicking. She knew crocodiles could move quickly. Surely she couldn't outswim it, but she would try. With everything in her, she kicked her legs and paddled her arms.

"It's getting closer!" Numu called. His voice was laced with panic.

Suddenly a current pushed around her. Her leg scraped against a rock, but she didn't feel any pain. The current shoved her closer to the raft. With one hand Numu clung to the vine he was holding, and with the other hand he reached out the steering stick toward her, long in the water.

Mesi refused to look back. She forced herself to keep moving. *Kick, kick, kick,* she told herself. *God, help me. Please!*

Numu pulled the stick out of the water. Was he giving up on her? Was he leaving? But he held the stick back over his shoulder like a javelin and threw it. Mesi felt the *whoosh* of the stick flying over her head, and then she heard a strange thud close behind her.

She turned to look. The crocodile veered his head up, stunned by the stick.

"Hurry, Mesi!" Numu called. "He'll come again in a minute, more angry than ever!"

Within seconds, Mesi grabbed Numu's hand and scrambled up to safety. They beached the rickety raft while Numu went to find another steering stick.

The crocodile came by, peered at them, and then moved along. Apparently he decided the pain wasn't worth it. Minutes later, Mesi and Numu were traveling on the river again.

Mesi flopped back on the raft in exhaustion. Her heart rate slowly returned to normal.

"I guess your god must have been looking the other way," Numu said.

"What do you mean?" said Mesi. "He saved me, didn't he?"

"*I'm* the one who threw the stick."

"And God's the one who gave you aim," said Mesi.

♡♡♡

Mesi's clothes were nearly dry as they floated closer to Numu's village.

"Only a few more minutes," Numu said when he started noticing familiar trees. "My family will be happy to meet you."

Mesi froze. What would her parents say if they knew she was so close to the Kienese village? With the recent threats, the villagers might hold her hostage. She would only cause trouble for her people if she were captured. "I can't go with you to your village, Numu," she said.

"Why not? They will want to reward you. To feed you a banquet. They will be so happy you took care of me and brought me home!"

Mesi swallowed. Perhaps they would reward her, but it wasn't worth the risk. "Numu, our villages are enemies."

Numu lodged his stick into some rocks to slow the raft and direct it toward the grassy shore. Waterberry trees hung their branches over the river, dropping purple berries with small splashes. "I will make sure they do nothing to harm you. Mesi, we are friends."

Mesi did trust Numu, but she could not trust his people. She waded into the water and scrambled up the muddy shore. "I must go." She looked up the hill and saw two shadowy figures in the distance. She would be found shortly if she stayed here. She could not waste a moment. "Goodbye, Numu."

"Mesi, wait!" he called. "I must thank you."

But already Mesi raced along the path. She needed to get as far from the Kienese village as possible. Numu could not run after her with his injuries.

She ran several hours, not feeling safe until she crossed the narrowest part of the river. Her village was located on this side. Everything looked familiar again, and she slowed her pace.

She'd done it. She'd returned Numu safely.

Now . . . if only no one asked any questions.

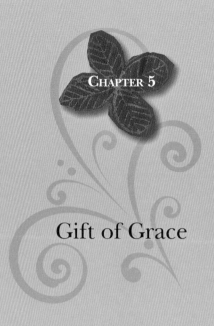

CHAPTER 5

Gift of Grace

Mesi's feet were burning by the time her homestead was in sight. She could see her mother stirring dinner in the black pot, with Jamilah swinging loosely on her back.

"Mother, may I help with anything?" she called.

Mother swung around and clicked her tongue on her teeth. "Mesi, Mesi. You've been gone all day. I hope you finished many of your doll clothes."

"It was a productive day," Mesi said carefully. She had hoped Mother would assume that she'd been down by the river, sewing all day.

Mother shook her head. "Next time do not be gone so long. You cannot do this business of yours and neglect your chores at home. They are your first responsibility."

"Yes, Mother. I'm sorry."

"Now hurry and get the water. Father will be back soon."

Mesi placed the urn on her head and almost ran into Shabot when she turned around. He was out of breath.

"Where's your father? Muleli, where's your husband?"

"In the field, Shabot. What is wrong?" Mother asked.

"Nothing! My boat has been returned."

Mesi was so stunned her head wobbled and the carefully balanced jug fell to the ground. Could it be that the Kienese returned it because she'd brought Numu home? Were they expressing their gratitude?

"The Kienese returned it?" asked Mother.

"Oh no," Shabot said. "Baka was telling the truth. His people didn't steal it. Some animal must have chewed the rope. It floated even further downstream."

"The waters have been high lately," Mother nodded.

"The Iluides found it, stuck in a beaver dam about fifteen kilometers south," he explained.

"Praise be," Mother said. "Yoofi will be so happy to hear it."

"He's coming now, Mother." Mesi pointed toward the horizon.

Father was riding the rusty blue bicycle with Kojo perched on the handlebars. He waved when he saw Shabot. Kojo put the bike away as Father greeted his friend with the traditional double-clasped handshake.

"Have you heard news of a drifter in the area?" he asked.

"No," Shabot said. "Why do you ask?"

"I went to check on the cow today, and I noticed someone had been staying in the shack. There was a blanket and left-over food. We watched all day but never saw anyone."

"Perhaps they noticed they'd been discovered and ran off," Shabot suggested.

"I wonder if they will return," Father said. "We have been talking about the possibility of the Kienese spying, perhaps hiding in the woods."

"In any case, we need to visit them again," Shabot said. "My boat has been found."

Father's eyebrows popped up, and Shabot explained what happened.

"Unfortunately, we've now stirred their anger," Father said.

After Shabot left, Mother added more wood to the fire, and Father began whittling at his spear. Kojo took out the *kikoga* game. He practiced putting the dried beans into the wooden cups as quickly as possible.

"Kojo, we'll need to be on guard," Father said. "We should go down late tonight and keep watch. See if this intruder returns."

Mesi quietly ground the millet. She didn't want her father to be worried, and she didn't want her brother to have to go out in the middle of the night to watch for someone she knew would not be returning. She had to tell the truth.

"Father," she said, "I know who was staying in the shack."

"What?" Father leaned forward, still clenching his spear. "Who was it? Why did you not tell us?"

Mesi hung her head. She could feel the stares of the other members of her family. "I found an injured boy down by the river a few days ago. He told me he was Kienese. I was worried he would be hurt by the people here, so I hid him while he recovered."

"You were taking care of a Kienese boy?" Father said.

"Yes, Father."

She heard her mother expel a big breath. "Mesi!"

47

"Do you realize the danger you put us in?" Father asked.

"I'm sorry. I did not mean to put anyone in danger," Mesi replied.

"You do not know if this was a spy. Where is he?"

"I took him back to his village this morning," she said.

"So that is where you were all day," Mother murmured.

"Yes," Mesi said. "We took Kojo's old raft."

"That load of sticks and putty! How in the world did you make it?" Father's voice remained laden with anger and disbelief.

"I fixed the raft."

"I'm very angry, Mesi. Very angry," Father said. "You put all of us in danger. The entire village. This boy could have been pretending. He could have been a spy to get close to the camp. He could have kidnapped you." He stood up and began to pace in front of the fire. "The Kienese could have found him and thought we kidnapped him. They would have come through and torched the village without asking any questions. Do you understand what you've done?"

Mesi hadn't. "I'm sorry, Father."

Mother finally had to speak. "And you know not to keep secrets from us. We are your parents. You do not deceive us."

"Go to bed now," Father said. "We will discuss your punishment tomorrow."

Mesi crawled into bed and ignored the growling of her stomach. It had been a long day and she was hungry, but there would be no dinner tonight.

♡♡♡

For two weeks Mesi was not allowed to leave the home-stead except for school. Father barely spoke to her. He was still angry, and she could understand why. But it was also frustrating for her—she'd only been trying to do what was right and what she thought God wanted her to do. Now she was uncertain.

Father also had taken away her responsibility of taking care of Lulu. That hurt the most—to know that Father no longer trusted her.

Mesi did everything she could to prove her contrition. She completed all her chores without being reminded and looked for extra ways to help out as well. But Father still barely spoke to her.

As she sat by the fire one day, patching Father's pants, she was surprised to hear Mother greet an old friend.

"Miss Ama, how good to see you. To what do we owe this visit?"

Mother bowed her head to Miss Ama as a sign of respect. Mesi stood up and did the same.

Miss Ama grabbed Mother's hand in her wrinkled grasp and squeezed it. "I have come to pay your daughter a visit."

Mother did not hide her surprise. "Mesi?"

"Yes."

"Did she cause trouble of some sort?"

"Oh no." Miss Ama laughed, and her crinkled eyes disappeared into her heavily lined forehead. "I would like to go for a walk with her, if that is all right with you?"

"Of course," Mother said. She wouldn't deny the request of the sage. The elderly were most worthy of respect.

Mesi fell into a slow step with Miss Ama. They walked in silence together for a long ways. Mesi did not feel she should say anything until Miss Ama spoke. The woman shuffled along with her walking stick and finally said, "I heard about your Kienese friend."

"His name was Numu," Mesi said. "I felt so badly for him. He was very hurt. I don't think he would have survived if I had left him."

"And you did not think he would be safe if you brought him back to the village," Miss Ama said.

"The cow shack seemed like the safest place," Mesi explained. "And keeping it a secret was the only option."

The two shuffled along in silence for a while longer. Miss Ama nodded at some of the other villagers working in their gardens and fetching water. After months of hiding under damp dirt, green sprouts everywhere reached toward the sun. The villagers nodded back to Miss Ama but avoided eye contact with Mesi. Everyone had heard about what happened. Everyone felt betrayed by her.

Mesi had one question. With her parents upset with her and the village angry with her, perhaps she would have been better off leaving Numu by the river. Maybe his people would have found him, and it would have saved her a lot of trouble.

"Miss Ama, I tried to offer grace to Numu. I really did. But now everyone is upset with me. Did I do the right thing?"

"What do you think?" she asked.

"I thought it was the right thing at the time. I remembered what you said about offering grace to people. But now that everyone is upset with me, I'm thinking maybe that doesn't apply to people who are your enemies."

Miss Ama paused and leaned on her walking stick. They were at the edge of the village, and the acacia trees formed a wall of shining, dancing leaves. Miss Ama stared up at them for a long time.

"In God's Word to us there is a story of a man who finds another injured man. Much like you did." She paused. "The injured man was from an enemy village."

"Did the other man help the injured one?" asked Mesi. She was stunned that there was another story like hers. And God had told it!

"He did. He gave him a place to stay and paid for his food and his treatment. He, like you, gave more than mercy." Miss Ama said.

"He gave grace," Mesi said.

"Yes, grace," Miss Ama said. "Grace like God gave you. God does not pick and choose who is worthy of grace and who is not. If that were true, no one would receive grace, yet he offers it to everyone. We should give grace as generously as he does."

"Not everyone sees it that way," said Mesi. "Kwasi certainly didn't. She thought we should turn him over to the elders. Or at least leave him where we found him."

Miss Ama nodded. "Not everyone has received grace, either—like you have. It is a hard thing to give what you've never received."

Mesi understood. Because God lived in her, she could offer the things of God.

The two continued to talk. As they headed through a line of trees, Miss Ama asked, "Do you see anything, child?"

Mesi looked past some hanging limbs. She blinked. There in the clearing, where she'd dreamed of building a church, was a massive tower of cinder blocks! This couldn't be real . . . but it was! "What? How? Who?" Mesi wasn't making any sense.

"There is a note," Miss Ama said, pointing.

Mesi jumped over the tall grasses and grabbed the white paper. She unfolded it.

MESI,

THANK YOU FOR SAVING MY LIFE. MY FAMILY AND MY PEOPLE ARE VERY GRATEFUL. AS YOU DID NOT LET US SHOW OUR GRATITUDE, I HOPE THIS WILL DEMONSTRATE IT. I'M STILL NOT SURE ABOUT THIS GOD OF YOURS. BUT I KNOW IT WAS HE WHO CAUSED YOU TO HELP ME. FOR THAT WE FEEL HE DESERVES A CHURCH.

YOUR FRIEND,
NUMU

Mesi read the note again, looked at the cinder blocks again, and read the note once more. She still couldn't believe it.

"When did you find this?" she asked Miss Ama, realizing this was the purpose of their mysterious walk.

"This morning," she said. "They must have come in the middle of the night."

"That was dangerous," Mesi said.

"Numu's family and his village must be very thankful, indeed," Miss Ama replied.

♡♡♡

Shabot and Uncle Yorkoo beat tall drums. Other people joined them on panpipes and kudu horns. Mesi's aunt tapped on the wooden keys of the *akadinda* alongside her four girls. Kwasi held hands with the other children in the village and circled around, singing folksongs. The rich smell of a roasting pig filled the room, the smoke slightly stinging Mesi's eyes. She breathed in deep.

"This is a wonderful celebration," said Numu, beside her.

Mesi nodded. It had actually been Chief Nbu's idea. After Mesi, Miss Ama, and her father explained everything to him, he took some men with him to walk down to the Kienese village. He offered them necklaces as an offering of peace, and they accepted. Chief Nbu promised the Kienese chief, Numu's father, that when the building was done the tribes would celebrate together. So tonight they'd all come, dressed regally in the brightest of colors, shaking hands and greeting their former enemies.

The men of Mesi's village had built the church quickly. They mixed mortar and stacked the blocks. And after a few weeks, large sheets of metal were laid over top. There wasn't a structure in the village as big or beautiful as the church. Children played soccer nearby and went inside when it got drizzly to play games protected from the rain.

There was still not a pastor, but on Sunday mornings, Miss Ama and Mesi met to pray. Miss Ama would read from her worn Bible. Sometimes Mesi's mother would join them. Other villagers were starting to come as well. Mesi invited Uncle Yorkoo to come, as she had promised, and he'd come a couple of times. The small group would sit in a circle and sing songs that Miss Ama taught them.

The church was beautiful, and so was tonight's celebration. Mesi noticed some of the older villagers—including Shabot and his family—hovered near the doorways, watching skeptically. But many of the villagers, especially the children, had embraced the Kienese.

"You started this, Mesi," Numu said. "You brought our people together."

Mesi watched a little Kienese girl dance around with her brother and some other village children, her blue cotton skirt flapping up and her eyes sparkling from the light of the torches that hung on the walls.

A new season had begun. Not only were father's cocoa plants blooming and ginger flowers opening in the savannah like bright orange suns, but new friendships were taking root as well.

"Thank you, Numu," she said. "But I believe it was God who brought us together."

In Step with Africa

Africa's Children

Forty-three percent of the continent's 900 million people are under the age of fifteen. In some African states, half or more of the population is under twenty-five.

Education

Education in Africa began as a tool to prepare young people to take their place in African society, not necessarily for life outside of Africa.

© 2007 iStock / Peeter Viisimaa

Africa has more than 40 million children, and almost half receive no schooling. Two-thirds of these are girls. There are still 46 million African children who have never stepped into a classroom.

© 2008 iStock / Liz Leyden

Africa's Geography
Making up one-fifth of the land mass of the earth, and with more than fifty countries, Africa's geographical features are diverse.

Rain Forest
There are tropical rain forests in nine countries of west Africa: Benin, Ghana, Guinea Bissau, Guinea, Ivory Coast, Liberia, Nigeria, Sierra Leone, and Togo.

Mountains
Kilimanjaro, in east Africa, is the tallest freestanding mountain in the world, rising 15,100 feet from its base.

Deserts

The Sahara Desert, in North Africa, is the world's second-largest desert, covering 3.5 million square miles—most of the northern part of the continent. It is almost as large as the continental United States.

59

African Wildlife

The African continent and its surrounding seas and islands are home to a diverse mix of animals, including more than one thousand different kinds of mammals. Some mammals prefer arid North Africa for their home, while others prefer west and central Africa's rain forest, which is home to numerous animals found nowhere else.

Gorilla

Gorillas are the largest of the living primates. Ground dwellers, they make their home in the tropical or subtropical forests of Africa.

Crocodile

Crocodiles are reptiles that live in the tropics of Africa. They are very fast over short distances, even out of the water. Their extremely powerful jaws give them a stronger bite than any other animal, more than five thousand pounds per square inch. The bite of a large great white shark exerts only four hundred pounds per square inch.

Lion

Lions are often referred to as the "king of the jungle." They are the second-largest living cat after the tiger. In Africa, lions can be found in savannah grasslands. The head of the male lion is one of the most widely recognized animal symbols in human culture.

Elephant

Elephants are the largest land animals alive today. There are three living species of elephants: the African bush elephant, the African forest elephant, and the Asian elephant, all ancestors of the extinct mammoth elephant.

Giraffe

The African giraffe is the tallest of all land animals. Males can be sixteen to eighteen feet tall. The giraffe is related to the deer and makes its home in savannas, grasslands, and open woodlands from Chad to the country of South Africa.

Zebra

Zebras are best known for their distinctive white and black stripes, which come in different patterns unique to each zebra. Zebras make their home in the eastern, southern, and south-western areas of Africa. Social animals, they can be seen in small harems to large herds.

Hippopotamus

Hippopotamuses, nick-named "hippos," are a large, mostly plant-eating mammal inhabiting rivers and lakes in sub-Saharan Africa . Hippos are recog-nizable for their barrel-shaped torso, enormous mouth and teeth, hairless body, stubby legs, and tremendous size. Despite their stocky shape and short legs, they can easily outrun humans and are regarded by some as Africa 's most dangerous animal.

We celebrate the strength and wisdom that we have in Christ, so today and into the future we can become all that God has purposed.

Girls 'n Grace 18" dolls have been beautifully sculpted by the renowned doll artist Dianna Effne

International characters!

Discover an international community of Girls 'n Grace from Africa, the United Kingdom, India, Peru, and more!

I Can Through Christ!®

Girls 'n Grace Like Me! Collection

Choose a doll that looks like you!

Choose your Girls 'n Grace doll today!

Each 18" Girls 'n Grace doll comes with:

 a doll-sized Bible with thirty-two verses on God's grace!

 a tag with a secret address code to an online virtual world —Girls 'n Grace Place!

 a designer box to store your doll and her accessories.

Visit www.GirlsnGrace.com **and register to win a free doll!**

Contemporary historical characters from the 1960s to the 1990s!

I Can Through Christ!®

Sydney Clair
1960s

Patrice
1960s

Mesi: A Girl 'n Grace in Africa

Mesi (pronounced *Maycee*) is a girl growing up on the continent of Africa. The landscape is as diverse as its people and their beliefs. Living in a village dependent on crops, Mesi's education and her family's well- being are in jeopardy when drought occurs. Through hardship, Mesi discovers a God who is near, so near that he cares about what concerns her. And she finds out about his inexhaustible treasure called grace.

Sydney Clair: A Girl 'n Grace in the 1960s

Sydney Clair Wilcox is a determined, curious ten-year-old trying to keep up with all the changes around her. The year is 1965. In the middle of the civil rights, women's rights, and environmental movements, Sydney discovers God's grace and how it makes her heart bloom.

Order online
www.GirlsnGrace.com

I Can Through Christ!®

Girls 'n Grace NIV New Testament

Girls 'n Grace offers an NIV New Testament with an attractive cover to attract this generation of reader. The NIV is the most widely accepted contemporary Bible translation today. This NIV New Testament was created to accurately and faithfully translate the original Greek, Hebrew, and Aramaic biblical texts into clearly understandable English.

Be sure and visit the Girls 'n Grace website for games, quizzes, prizes, and more!

www.GirlsnGrace.com

In Touch With God in Africa

Refraining from punishment is mercy. Giving an undeserved gift is grace.

READ HEBREWS 4:15–16. Does God want us to come to him to receive mercy and grace? _____

_____

_____

When we receive God's mercy and grace, then we can extend mercy and grace to others.

READ 1 PETER 3:8–9. Had Mesi received God's mercy and grace? Was she blessed in sharing it? _____

_____

_____

When people are unkind, it reveals they are poor in God's grace.

READ MATTHEW 6:19–21. What are some treasures that people seek in place of God and his grace? _____

_____

_____

To possess a treasure, you must first seek it.

READ JEREMIAH 29:13. Does God want you to find him and the treasure of his grace? What will it require for you to find it?

_____

_____

_____

Share this book and God's love with a friend, so she can know the love and grace of God. To learn more about God's inexhaustible treasure of grace, go to www.GirlsnGrace.com/GraceNow.html.